This book belongs to:

____

OPERATION Laughter

written by
Dawn Renee Young

illustrated by
Abigail Powers

Library of Congress Control Number: 2024913582

Book Design – Sharon Kizziah-Holmes

Published by

SOLANDER
PRESS
Springdale, Arkansas

Paperback ISBN 13: 978-1-959548-56-0
Hardback ISBN 13: 978-1-959548-57-7
eBook ISNB 13: 978-1-959548-58-4

CONTENTS

1

THE JOKE-TELLER

Millie returned home from spending her spring break with Grandma and Grandpa. She loved her alone time with the two of them. Sometimes, a girl needed a break away from bossy and clingy brothers.

Her favorite parts of her trip were Grandma's homemade chocolate chip cookies and snuggly hugs. She enjoyed laughing at Grandpa's silly jokes. Millie loved to laugh.

Grandpa said, “Laughing is good for the soul.” He was the best joke-teller.

Crawling into her own cozy bed, Millie had an idea. *What if I could make people laugh? I’m going to be a joke-teller, just like Grandpa.*

At breakfast, mission Operation Laughter began.

Millie’s little brother, Charlie, was quieter than usual.

“What’s wrong?” Millie asked.

"I had a bad dream."

Millie hugged him and said, "I ate a ten-pound marshmallow in my dream."

"Really?" he asked.

"When I woke up, my pillow was gone."

Charlie's eyes sparkled as he giggled.

"Do you know why eggs don't tell jokes?"

"I don't know. Why?" Charlie answered with a mouth full of cereal.

"Because they would crack themselves up!" Millie laughed and laughed.

Charlie laughed, too! Her older brother,

Jack, rolled his eyes.

Operation Laughter was underway. One laugh was better than none.

2

BUS LAUGHS

Millie hurried down the street to her bus stop. She couldn't wait to share jokes with her two best friends.

"Hey, Ming," she said. "I'm excited to

hear about everyone's spring break and projects today."

"I'm scared to talk in front of the class," Ming whispered.

"You'll do great," Millie said. "What did the shy pebble wish?"

"I don't know."

"She wished to be a little boulder." Millie giggled.

Ming thought for a moment and giggled, too.

"I'll try to be bold like you, Millie," Ming said.

"You'll do great!" Millie reassured her friend.

"Thanks, Millie. Here comes our bus."

Millie climbed the bus steps, greeting Ms. Thomas, their bus driver.

"Hi, Ms. Thomas."

"Good morning, Millie."

"What's yellow, has thirty-eight eyes, and

can't swim?" she asked her.

Ms. Thomas smiled. "You got me."

"A school bus."

Ms. Thomas laughed and told Millie it was time to sit down.

Millie hurried to the back seat. Millie's other best friend, Kera, saved Ming and Millie seats every morning. Millie plopped down, and the three girls discussed their spring break.

As they neared the school, Millie asked,

"Do you know what elves learn at school?"

"No, but I bet you will tell us." Ming giggled.

"The elf-abet." Millie laughed and laughed.

Kera threw her head back and laughed so hard she snorted. Millie wondered if she could make Mrs. Jones, her teacher, laugh.

3

CLASSROOM COMEDY

Millie bounced into her classroom. She quickly unloaded her backpack and hung up her coat. She couldn't wait to try to get a laugh out of Mrs. Jones.

"Good morning, Mrs. Jones."

"Good morning, Millie."

"Why do teachers wear sunglasses?"

"Because our students are so bright," Mrs. Jones answered, grinning.

I'll think of another teacher joke and stump her next time, thought Millie.

"Class, please take out your math books."

Millie stood up. "What do books do in the winter?"

The class was quiet. Ming stared at Mille. She couldn't believe Millie was interrupting class.

"They put on their jackets." Millie laughed and laughed.

John, Kera, and Diego laughed, too.

"Good one, Millie," John said.

That joke was a hit! Millie tried another

one. "Where do pencils go on vacation?"

"Millie, that's enough," Mrs. Jones said.

Millie whispered, "Pencil-vania."

Sara giggled.

In social studies, Millie passed a written joke to Sami, who passed it to Diego, who passed it to Amanda. By the time social studies was over, all of her classmates had read the joke. Tiny hee-hee-hees spread throughout the room. Millie planned to try her luck at lunch.

4

CAFETERIA GIGGLES

Millie's belly began to grumble. *It must be getting close to lunchtime*, she thought to herself. Glancing at the clock, she noticed she was right. She couldn't wait. The best part wasn't going to be the food today. She was going to tell jokes.

Pushing her tray along the cafeteria line, Millie asked Miss Ida, the cafeteria lady, "What do cats call mice on skateboards?"

"I don't know, Little Miss Joke-teller. What?"

"Meals on wheels."

Miss Ida threw her head back and belted out a belly laugh.

When Millie reached the table where Ming and Kera were sitting, she stuck to her plan.

She placed her tray on the table. "What's in an astronaut's favorite sandwich?"

"We give up," Kera said.

"Launch meat."

Everyone at the table laughed.

That went well. She'd try again.

"What do you get when you put three ducks in a box?"

"I know, a box of ducks," John said.

"No, silly. a box of quackers."

"That's lame," John complained.

"Hey, Diego, why did the student eat his homework?"

"I have no idea, Millie. Why?"

"The teacher told him it was a piece of cake."

Shrieks exploded into the air.

Operation Laughter was underway.

5

MR. BAKER

Mr. Baker, the lunch monitor, glided toward Millie's table.

"What's so funny over here?"

Everyone pointed at Millie.

"Millie, what are you up to?" Mr. Baker asked.

"Not much. Just eating my lunch and telling a few jokes," she said.

After taking a bite of her spaghetti, Millie asked, "Mr. Baker, do you know why fish avoid the computer?"

"No, Millie. Why?"

"So they don't get caught in the internet."

Laughter erupted throughout the cafeteria.

Diego said, "Millie, tell him the one about the elephant and the refrigerator."

"How can you tell if an elephant has been in your refrigerator?" she asked.

Mr. Baker smiled. "Footprints in the cheesecake. My nephew told me that one.

"Okay, enough jokes. It's almost time to get back to class."

The class cleaned up their lunch mess and lined up along the wall.

Waiting for Mrs. Jones, Millie stepped out of line and asked, “When potatoes have babies, what are they called? Anyone? Anyone? Tater tots.”

She laughed and laughed. Diego doubled over with laughter.

Mrs. Jones heard loud chuckles as she

entered the cafeteria. She looked at her class and shook her head. "Millie the joke-teller must be at it again."

Millie couldn't believe how many laughs she got at lunchtime.

6

DINNER TIME

Mom set salmon, French fries, and coleslaw on the table for dinner.

"That smells yummy," Millie said.

The salmon reminded her of another joke. "Why do fish live in salt water?" she asked.

Dad began to explain, but Millie interrupted, "Because pepper makes them sneeze."

Her brothers cackled. Dad didn't think it was funny.

"I received an email from Mrs. Jones today," Mom said.

"I bet she told you what a good joke-teller I am," Millie said.

"Not exactly," Mom said. "Mrs. Jones said that you told jokes all day long, interrupting learning."

"Yeah, I did. It was great."

"Millie, part of telling jokes is to understand *when* to tell jokes. Interrupting the class isn't the right way to do it," Mom said.

"You are at school to learn, not tell jokes," Dad said.

"But I like to make people laugh, just like Grandpa. Remember, Grandpa always says, 'Laughter is good for the soul!'"

Millie hesitated. "I'll try harder not to interrupt class, but I'm still going to be a joke-teller."

Charlie looked at his family and asked, "What's a potato's favorite animal?"

"Not you, too," Dad said. "One joke-teller

in the family is enough."

"We give up," Millie said.

"An alli-tator." Charlie chuckled.

"That was a good one, Charlie," Millie said, patting her little brother on the back.

Dad just shook his head.

Millie wondered how she could still be a joke-teller, keep Operation Laughter

going, and figure out the right times to tell jokes.

7

SOFTBALL PRACTICE

Millie helped Mom clear the table and clean up after dinner.

She hurried when she remembered she had softball practice that night.

Dad came into the kitchen. "Millie, grab your bat and glove. It's time to leave for softball practice."

Millie raced up the steps to her room. She grabbed her gear and headed back down to the car.

Buckling her seat belt, Millie asked, "Dad, where does a softball player go when he needs a new uniform?"

"He probably goes to a sporting goods store," Dad said.

"Nooo. New Jersey." Millie cackled.

"Girl, you need to start thinking about softball, not jokes."

As they entered the parking lot to the ballpark, she asked, "Do you know what one of the softball players did when Coach said to steal second?"

"No, what?"

"He picked up the base and went home." She giggled.

Dad shook his head. "Millie, please listen to Coach and follow directions tonight.

Coach is giving up his valuable time to help you girls. Mom will pick you up after practice."

"Love you," she said, blowing Dad a kiss.

"Love you, too, pumpkin."

Millie raced to the field. Millie couldn't wait to tell Coach a joke.

8

COACH

Millie plopped her bag on the bench. She was thinking about all the jokes she was going to tell during practice.

Coach asked, "How's my first base girl today?"

"Good." Millie couldn't hold it in any longer. "Hey, Coach, why are softball players so rich?"

Coach pondered a moment and said, "Because they work hard and never give up."

Millie smirked. "Nooo. Because they play on diamonds!"

"Okay, Millie, take your base."

The team took their outfield positions. Coach hit several fly balls at them.

"Bring it in!" Coach shouted.

Sara and Millie were running toward home plate. Suddenly, Sara slipped and twisted her ankle in a hole.

Millie stopped and shouted to Coach, “Please come quick! Sara fell and twisted her ankle. She’s crying.”

Coach ran out onto the field and examined Sara’s ankle and foot. “We’d better call your parents. You may need to get some X-rays,” Coach said, carrying

Sara to the dugout.

Millie sat down on the bench beside Sara. She hated that her friend was hurt.

She had an idea. *I'll tell her a joke to make her feel better.*

"What do softball players eat on?"

"Oh no, not another joke," Sara said, tears dripping down her face.

"Home plates, of course."

Sara giggled through her tears.

Millie sat with Sara until her parents picked her up. After Sara left, Coach gathered the team for a pep talk.

"Tomorrow night we are going to practice our batting," Coach told the team.

"Any questions?"

Millie raised her hand.

"Yes, Millie?"

"Where should a softball player never wear red?"

Coach got a serious look on his face.

Millie knew she had pushed her luck, but she couldn't help herself. "In the bull pen."

The whole team burst into laughter.

Coach wasn't happy. "Millie, this isn't the time for jokes. Take a lap."

As Millie ran her lap, she realized she had pushed her joke-telling limit with Coach.

"I'm sorry, Coach. I'll try to pay more attention."

"Good idea, Millie," Coach said.

Millie didn't know whether to tell her parents about the extra lap.

9

RIDE HOME

Millie saw Mom pull up and park by the field. She told her teammates goodbye and ran over to the car.

Throwing her bag in the backseat, Mom asked, "How was practice?"

"Not good. Sara fell and hurt her ankle. Her parents had to come and pick her up. I hope she is okay."

"So do I," Mom said.

Millie lowered her head and whispered, "And I think I told too many jokes. Coach made me run an extra lap."

"I thought we talked about the right and wrong times to tell jokes."

Millie said, "We did. I did make Sara feel better when she fell and hurt her ankle."

"That's good," Mom said.

"I told her a joke," Millie said. "Mom, do you know what softball has in common with pancakes?"

"This better not be a joke, Millie," Mom

said sternly.

Millie shook her head and said, “Never mind.”

They both rely on the batter.

“Millie, when we get home, I want you to get ready for bed.”

“I will. Can I please read for twenty minutes before bed?”

"Yes, then lights out," Mom said.

Millie couldn't wait to read her new joke book she'd checked out of the library.

10

GOOD NIGHT GRANDPA

Ring-ring-ring.

"Hello," Millie said, grabbing the phone between reading pages of jokes.

"How's my little marvelous Millie?" Grandpa asked.

"I'm good. I told a lot of jokes today. My friends loved them. Mrs. Jones, not so much."

"Why is that?" Grandpa asked.

"I interrupted class a little."

"Remember, a good joke-teller knows when to tell them. It's okay to tell jokes on the bus, at recess, and lunchtime. But you should never interrupt your teacher when she is teaching class."

"I'll try to remember."

She told him about Sara getting hurt. But she left out the part about running the extra lap.

"What did the Gingerbread Man put on

his bed?" Grandpa asked,

"I give up."

"A cookie sheet."

They both laughed.

"Grandpa, do you know what you call Grandpa and Grandma on speed dial?"

"No, Millie, I don't."

"Insta-Grams." She giggled.

"Sweet dreams, my sweet joke-teller. Love you," Grandpa said.

"Love you, too."

Tomorrow, Operation Laughter, Part Two.

About the Author

Dawn Renee Young earned her doctorate in Education. She has always worked with children as an elementary teacher, principal, TEAM Evaluator, and reading specialist. She is currently a full-time children's author. Her debut picture book was The ABCs of Making Good Choices. She has written seven books in the Mrs. Good Choice Series. Her books have won numerous awards, including Reader's Choice and Mom's Choice.

Her other picture books include:

TAP-TAP-TAP (Solander Press)

Little Cub's Big List, Fun with Sight Words (Solander Press)

The ABCs of God's Great Love (Thomas Nelson- Christian)

Liam's Big Surprise (Solander Press)

Loose at the Zoo (Solander Press)

One of Dawn's greatest joys is engaging with her young readers. She loves making school visits and attending other child-focused events where she can share her love for reading and writing. Dawn and her husband currently reside near Nashville, TN.

https://mrsgoodchoice.com

@MrsGoodchoice

dawn@mrsgoodchoice.com

About the Illustrator

Abigail Powers, is an artist and graphic designer from Michigan. She spent the early years of her career working in graphic design and as a K-12 art educator. In 2020, she found herself at home with her kids riding out the pandemic. Abby picked up her paint brushes and began to create art for the sake of creating art...getting back to what she always loved most, creating!

From this, Abigail Leigh Designs, was born. In the last two years the business has kept Abigail very busy and the best part has been working on so many different projects. In the past two years the business has grown through markets, art fairs, websites, local clients and so much more. Illustrating children's books was always a dream and meeting author, Dawn Young, made it a reality.

Made in the USA
Columbia, SC
06 August 2024

39587975R00028